The Wheel Of Life
Part IV
Reconciliation

by

Ellen Glasgow

Double9 BOOKS

The Wheel Of Life
Part IV
Reconciliation
by Ellen Glasgow

ISBN: 978-93-64282-98-7

Published by

DOUBLE 9 BOOKS
2/13-B, Ansari Road
Daryaganj, New Delhi – 110002
info@double9books.com
www.double9books.com
Tel. 011-40042856

ABOUT THE AUTHOR

Ellen Glasgow (1873–1945) was an influential American novelist who chronicled the social and cultural changes in the American South during the late 19th and early 20th centuries. Here are some key aspects of her life and work. Glasgow published her first novel, "The Descendant," in 1897 under the pseudonym "Ellen Glasgow." The novel's exploration of heredity and environment set the tone for her later works. Her novels often dealt with themes such as the decline of the Southern aristocracy, the rise of industrialism, the role of women in society, and the conflicts between tradition and progress. Some of her most significant novels include "Virginia" (1913), "Barren Ground" (1925), "The Sheltered Life" (1932), and "In This Our Life" (1941), which won the Pulitzer Prize for Fiction in 1942. Ellen Glasgow is regarded as one of the leading Southern writers of her time. Her work has been praised for its insight into the changing Southern society and its strong, independent female characters. Ellen Glasgow died on November 21, 1945, in Richmond, Virginia. Her contributions to American literature have continued to be celebrated, and her novels remain an important part of the canon of Southern literature. Ellen Glasgow's keen observations and nuanced portrayals of Southern life have left a lasting impact on American literature, making her an essential figure in the study of the South's cultural and social evolution.

CONTENTS

CHAPTER I
THE SECRET CHAMBERS

Waking in the night, with a start, Laura asked herself why she had burned the letter. As she lay there in the darkness it seemed to her that the sudden light shone in her thoughts again, and she saw everything made clear to her as she had seen it while she held Jennie Alta's hand. In that instant she had looked beyond the small personal emotions to the woman's soul with its burden of greed and sensuality, and because she had been able to do this, she had felt herself to be composed and released from hatred. To discern the soul was to feel not only tolerance, but pity for the flesh, and it appeared to her now that in that one moment she had ceased to be herself alone, and had shared in the divine wisdom which the sudden light had revealed to her in her breast. Yet the instant afterward her personality had triumphed and she had burned the letter!

The illumination within her faded now, and as she lay there with wide open eyes, she saw only the surrounding darkness. Her own motives were still vague to her; when she tried to remember the prompting of her thoughts she could recall only a physical pain which had entered her bosom while she looked at the large white envelope upon the blotter. "Before this I had never lied in my life," she said, "I had never been capable of the slightest dishonest act, I had even taken a pride in my truth like the pride some women take in beauty—and yet I did this thing without effort and I do not know now why I did, nor what I thought of at the time, nor whether I regretted it the moment afterward."

With a resolution which had seldom failed her, she attempted to banish the recollection from her mind; and turning her face from the pale darkness of the window, she closed her eyes again and lay breathing quietly. "Why should I worry—it will all come right—everything will come right if I have patience," she thought, trying to persuade herself to sleep.

But she had no sooner shut her eyes than she began to live over again the afternoon in Kemper's room; and her heart beat so high that she heard the muffled sound under the coverlet "Why did Gerty look at me so?" she asked. "Did she really look at me as if she were afraid, or was it only my imagination?" From Gerty her excited thoughts flew back to Kemper and it seemed to her that she had read scorn and suspicion in the beaming glance he had thrown upon her—in the breathless apology of his entrance. "Had he met her downstairs? Did he know all the time? and was he only waiting for Gerty's absence to accuse me face to face of my dishonesty? But it was a very little thing," she argued aloud, as if justifying herself to a presence beside her bed, "it was such a little thing that it had almost escaped my memory." Then, as she uttered the words, she realised that the justification she attempted was for her own soul rather than for her lover; and she saw that whether Kemper suspected or not made no vital difference to her so long as the dishonesty was there. "The unspoken lie is still between us and his knowledge of it can neither take it away nor undo the fact that it has been. And if I burned the letter might I not be guilty of even greater things under the same impulse? Since I trust neither him nor myself what is there but misery in any future that we may share? Shall I give him up even now? Can I give him up?" But as she demanded this of herself there returned to her the look in his eyes at certain animated instants, and she felt that the charm of his look, which meant nothing, was stronger to hold her than a multitude of reasons. "If I could forget this look in his face, I might forget him," she thought, "but though I struggle to forget it I cannot any more than I can forget the letter lying on his desk."

Again she closed her eyes in a fresh effort to shut out consciousness; but when she determined to sleep the darkness seemed to grow suddenly alive about her, and starting up in a spasm of terror, she lighted the candle on the table beside her bed.

"In the morning I shall tell him," she exclaimed aloud, "I shall tell him everything and if he looks at me with anger I shall go away and not see him any more." At the time it appeared to her very easy, and she felt that it made no difference to her however things might happen on the morrow. "It will be as it will be, and I cannot alter it, for in any event I shall be miserable whether I marry him or give him up." Then she remembered that though she had pardoned Kemper greater sins than this, by the courage of his attitude he had always succeeded in placing her hopelessly in the wrong. "Even after his meeting with Madame Alta it was he who forgave me," she thought with the strange mental clearness, which destroyed her happiness without lessening her emotion, "and through his whole life, however deeply he may wrong me, I know that I shall always be the one to justify myself and seek forgiveness. Is it, after all, only necessary to have the courage of one's acts that one may do anything and not be punished?"

The light of the candle flickering on the mirror gave back her own face to her as if reflected in the dim surface of a pool. She watched the shadows from a vase, of autumn leaves come and go across it, until it seemed to her that the rippling reflection resembled a drowned face that was still her own;

and shrinking back in horror, she sat holding the candle in her hand, so that the light would shine on the walls and floor.

"Yes, that is settled—I shall tell him to-morrow," she said, as if surrendering her future into the power of chance or God or whatever stood outside herself, "it will happen as it must, I cannot change it." For a moment there was some comfort in the fatalism of this thought, and after blowing out the candle, she turned her face to the wall and fell at last into a troubled sleep. But her sleep even was filled with perplexing questions, which she continued to ask herself with the same piercing mental clearness that tormented her when she was awake; and she passed presently into a vivid dream, in which she rescued the letter with burned hands, from the fire, and carried it to Kemper, who laughed and kissed her burns and threw the letter back into the flames. "It has never really happened—you have imagined it all," he said, "you've dreamed Jennie Alta and now you're dreaming me and yourself also. Look up, for you are just beginning to awake." And when she looked up at his words, his face changed suddenly and she saw that it was Roger Adams who held her hands.

From this dream she awoke with a more distinct memory of Adams than she had had for many days; and she felt again the impulse to unburden her heart to him, which she had resisted on the afternoon they walked together down Fifth Avenue. The dawn had begun to break, and while she waited impatiently for the growing light, she resolved with one of those promptings of wisdom, in which ordinary reason appeared to have no part, that when the morning came she would go to Adams' office before seeing Kemper. Then she remembered the distance which had sprung between them in the last few months, and it seemed to her to have grown still more impassable since the evening before. But because the visit offered an excuse to postpone her confession to Kemper until the afternoon, she caught at it with an eagerness, which hurried her into her hat and coat as soon as her pretence of breakfasting with Angela was at an end.

The morning was bright and clear, and as she walked through the early sunshine in the street, she remembered the day, so long ago now, when she had met Adams going to his office at this hour, and she recalled, with a smile, that she had pitied him then because of the worn places on his overcoat. She no longer pitied him now—Gerty, herself, Perry Bridewell, even Kemper, she felt, might be deserving of compassion, but not Adams. Yes, she, herself, in spite of her boasted strength had come at last to feel the need of being loved for the very weakness she had once despised. But she knew that, though Adams might understand and forgive this weakness, in Kemper it would provoke only the scorn which she had begun to fear and dread. Yet her intellect rather than her heart told her that Adams was a stronger man than Kemper and that his wider sympathies proved only that he was, also, the larger of the two. Was the difference between them merely one of goodness, after all, her intellect, not her heart, demanded, and was it true that the perfect love could not enter except where this goodness had been to blaze the way before it in the soul?

As she walked through the streets fanciful comparisons between the two men thronged in her brain, but when presently she reached Adams' office, and stood beside his desk, with her hand in his hearty grasp, she realised all at once that the visit was useless, and that there was nothing she could say to him which would not sound hysterical and absurd.

"So, thank heaven, there's something I can do for you!" he exclaimed, with his cordial smile. "Wait till I get into my overcoat and then we'll see about it."

"No—no," she protested in a terror, which she could not explain even to herself, "don't come out with me—there's nothing you can do. I came because I couldn't help myself," she added, smiling; "and I'll go for no better reason, in a little while."

"Well, I'm ready whenever you say so. If it's to overturn Brooklyn Bridge, I'll set about it for the asking."

"It isn't anything so serious—there's nothing really I want done," she answered gayly, though the pain in her eyes stabbed him to the heart, "all I wanted was to make sure of you—to make sure, I mean, that you are really here."

"Oh, I'm here all right!" he replied, with energy. She looked at him steadily for a moment with her excited eyes which had grown darkly brilliant.

"Do you know what I sometimes think?" she said, breaking into a pathetic little laugh, "it is that I remind myself of one of those angels who, after falling out of heaven, could neither get back again nor reconcile themselves to the things of earth."

Her hand lay on his desk, and while she spoke he bent forward and touched it an instant with his own. Light as the gesture was, it possessed a peculiar power of sympathy; and she was conscious as he looked at her that there was no further need for her to speak, because he understood, not only all that she had meant to put into words, but everything that was hidden in her heart as well.

"I can't preach to you, Laura," he said, "but—but—oh, I can't express even what is in my mind," he added. "I wish I could!"

"It wouldn't help me," she replied, "because although I am not reconciled with the things of earth I want to be—oh, how I want to be!"

"But you can't be—not you," he said. "You're of that particular fibre which grows stronger through pain, I think—and, in the end, how much easier it is to be made all spirit or all clay—it's the combination, not the pure quantity that hurts."

"I wonder if you ever know what it is?" she rejoined. "Does the earth ever pull you back when you want to climb?"

His smile faded, and he looked at her again with the sympathy which accepted, without explanation, not only her outward aspect, but the soul within. "There's not much in my life that counts for a great deal, Laura," he said, "but you come in for considerably the larger share of it. At this moment I am ready to do either of two things, as you may wish—I am ready to stand aside and let your future settle itself as it probably will, or I am ready, at your word, to hear everything and to judge for you as I would judge for myself. No—no, don't answer me now," he added, "carry it away with you, and remember or forget it, as you choose."

Though there were tears in her eyes as she looked at him, she turned away, after an instant, with a flippant laugh.

"Why, it all sounds as if I were really unhappy!" she exclaimed, "but you won't believe that, will you?"

"I'll gladly believe otherwise when you prove it."

"But haven't I proved it? Don't I prove it every day I live?"

"You prove to me at this minute that you are particularly wretched," he returned.

"I am not—I am not," she retorted angrily, while a frown drew her dark brows together. "You have no right to think such things of me—they are not true."

"I have a right to think anything that occurs to me," he corrected quietly, "though I am willing to beg your pardon for putting it into words. Well, since you assure me that you are entirely happy, I can only say that I am overjoyed to hear it."

"I am happy," she insisted passionately; and a little later when she was alone in the street, she told herself that a lie had become more familiar to her than the truth. The conversation with Adams appeared a mistake when she looked back upon it—for instead of lessening it seemed only to increase the weight of her troubles—so she determined presently to think no more either of Adams or of the reasons which had prompted her impulsive visit to him. To forget oneself! Yes, Gerty was right in the end, and the object of all society, all occupations, all amusements, showed to her now as so many unsuccessful attempts to escape the haunting particular curse of personality. Gerty escaped it by her frivolous pursuits and her interminable flirtations, which meant nothing; Kemper escaped it by living purely in the objective world of sense; Adams escaped it—The name checked her abruptly, and she stopped in her thoughts as if a light had flashed suddenly before her eyes. Here, at last, was the explanation of happiness, she felt, and yet she felt also, that it presented itself to her mind in an enigma which she could not solve—for Adams, she recognised, had mastered, not escaped, his personality. The poison of bitterness was gone, but the effectiveness of power was still as great; and his temperament, in passing through the fiery waters of experience, was mellowed into a charm which seemed less a fortunate grace of aspect than the result of a peculiar quality of vision. Was it his own life that had opened his eyes until he could look into the secret chambers in the lives of others?

In Gramercy Park she found Mrs. Payne waiting for her with the carriage, and she accepted almost eagerly the old lady's invitation to spend the morning in a search for hats. At the moment it seemed to her that hats offered as promising an aid to forgetfulness as any other, and she threw herself immediately into the pursuit of them with an excitement which enabled her, for the time, at least, to extinguish the fierce hunger of her soul in supplying the more visible exactions of her body.

At luncheon Gerty appeared, wearing a startling French gown, which, she said, had just arrived that morning. After the first casual greeting they fell into an animated discussion of the choice of veils, during which Gerty declared that Laura had never selected the particular spots which would be most becoming to her features. "You get them too large and too far apart," she insisted, picking up a black net veil from a pile on Laura's table, "even I with my silly nose can't stand this kind."

Laura's eyes were fixed upon her with their singular intensity of look, but in spite of the absorption of her gaze, she had not heard a single word that Gerty uttered.

"Yes, yes, you're right," she said; but instead of thinking of the veils, she was wondering all the time if Gerty had really forgotten her jealousy of Madame Alta and the letter she had burned.

"I shall tell him this afternoon and that will make everything easy," she thought; and when, after a little frivolous conversation Gerty had remembered an engagement and driven hurriedly away, the situation appeared to Laura to have become perfectly smooth again. At the announcement of Kemper's name, she crossed the room to meet him with this impulse still struggling for expression. "I shall tell him now, and then everything will be made easy," she repeated.

But when she opened her lips to speak, she found that the confession would not come into words, and what she really said was:

"It has been a century since yesterday, for I've done nothing but shop."

Laughing he caught her hands, and she saw with her first glance, that he was in one of his ironic moods.

"I thought I'd netted a wren," he answered, "but it seems I've caught a bird of Paradise."

"Then it was your ignorance of natural history, and not I, that deceived you," she retorted gayly, "because I didn't spread my wings for you, did you imagine that they were not brilliant?"

There was a note almost of relief in her voice as she spoke—for she knew now that, so long as he refused to be serious, she could not tell him until to-morrow.

CHAPTER II
IN WHICH LAURA ENTERS THE VALLEY OF HUMILIATION

Two weeks later Laura was still able to assure herself that it was this lack of "seriousness" in Kemper's manner which had kept her from alluding to the burned letter. Since the morning on which she had seen Adams, she felt that she had merely skimmed experience without actually touching it; and three days from the date of her marriage she was as far from any deeper understanding of the situation as she had been in the beginning of her love. In the end it was so much easier to ignore her difficulties than to face them; and it seemed to her now that she was forced almost in spite of herself into Gerty's frivolous attitude toward life. To evade the real—to crowd one's existence with little lies until there was no space left through which the larger truth might enter—this was the only solution which she had found ready for her immediate need.

Adams she had not met again; once he had called, but impelled by a shrinking which was almost one of fear, she had turned back on the threshold and refused to see him. Even Gerty she had tried to avoid since the afternoon in Kemper's rooms, but Gerty, who was in her gayest mood, drove down every day "to overturn," as she carelessly remarked, "the newest presents."

"I'm heartily glad you're going to Europe," she said, "and I hope by the time you come back you'll have lost that nervous look in your face. It never used to be there and I don't like it."

At her words Laura threw an alarmed glance at the mirror; then she turned her head with a laugh in which there was a note of bitterness.

"It came there in my effort to make conversation," she answered. "I've been engaged to Arnold eight months and we've talked out every subject that we have in common. Do you know what it is to be in love with a man and yet to rack your brain for something to say to him?" she finished merrily.

"That's because you ought to have married Roger Adams, as I was the only one to suggest," retorted Gerty, "then you'd have had conversation enough to flow on, without a pause, till Judgment Day. It's a very good thing, too," she added seriously, "because the real bug-a-boo of marriage is boredom, you know."

"But how can two people bore each other when they are in love?" demanded Laura, almost indignant.

The possibility appeared to her at the moment as little short of ridiculous, yet she knew, in her heart of hearts, that she faced, not without approaching dread, the thought of those two months in Europe; and she admitted now for the first time that beyond the absorption of their love, she and Kemper had hardly an interest which they shared. Even the eyes with which they looked on Europe would be divided by the space of that whole inner world which stretched between them. Yet because of the supremacy of this one sentiment she had striven to crush out her brain in order that she might have the larger heart with which to nourish the emotion which held them together. In the pauses of this sentiment she realised that their thoughts sprang as far asunder as the poles, and as she looked from Gerty to the wedding presents scattered in satin boxes on chairs and tables, the fact that the step she took was irrevocable, that in three days she would be Kemper's wife, that there was no possible escape from it now, produced a sudden sickening terror in her heart. Then with a desperate clutch at her old fatalistic comfort, she told herself that it would all come right if she were only patient—that with her marriage everything would be settled and become entirely simple.

Gerty was unpacking a case from a silversmith's when Kemper came in; and he gave a low whistle of dismay as he glanced about the room strewn with boxes.

"By Jove, I believe they think we're going to set up a business!" he exclaimed.

"Oh, you can't imagine how all this comes in for entertaining," replied Gerty, shaking out her skirt as she rose from her knees.

Laura's eyes were on Kemper's face, and she saw that it wore a look of annoyance beneath the conventional smile with which he responded to Gerty's words. Something had evidently happened to displease him, and she waited a little anxiously half hoping for, half dreading her friend's departure.

"I trust you'll go through the ceremony more gracefully than Perry did," Gerty was saying with a teasing merriment, while she broke a white rosebud from the vase of flowers and fastened it in his coat. "I declare he quite spoiled the whole effect, he looked so frightened. I never realised how little sense of humour Perry has until I saw him at the altar."

"Well, it isn't exactly a joke, you know," retorted Kemper.

For the first time, as Laura watched him, she remembered that he had been through it all before without her; and the thought entered her heart like a dagger, that even now there was another woman alive somewhere in the world who had been his wife—who had been almost as much loved, almost as close to him as she herself was to-day. The thought sickened her, and she felt again her blind terror of a step so irrevocable.

Gerty had gone at last; and Kemper, after walking twice up and down the room, stopped to examine a silver coffee service with an attention which was so evidently assumed that Laura was convinced he might as well have fixed his gaze upon the fireplace. His thoughts were busily occupied in quite an opposite direction from his eyes, for turning presently, he laid down the sugar bowl he had picked up, and went rapidly to the mantel piece, where he took down a photograph of Roger Adams.

"You don't see much of Adams now?" he remarked enquiringly.

"Not much," she went over to the mantel and glanced carelessly at the picture in his hand. "I never shall again."

"How's that? and why?"

"Oh, I don't know—one never sees much of one's friends after marriage, somehow. To supply the world to me," she added gayly, "is a part of the responsibility of your position."

Though his gaze was fixed intently upon her face, she saw clearly that he had hardly taken in her words, for while she spoke his hands wandered to the inside pocket of his coat, as if he wished to make sure of a letter he had placed there.

"By the way, Laura, a queer thing happened to-day," he said, frowning.

She looked up a little startled.

"A queer thing?"

"I had a letter from Madame Alta asking why I hadn't sold some stock I'd been holding for her? She lost a good deal by my not selling and she was in a devilish temper about it."

Laura had not lowered her eyes, and as he finished she smiled into his face.

"And you did not sell?" she asked.

"I never got the letter—but the odd part is she says she came to see me about it the day you were there with Gerty—that she saw you and that she left the letter with you to deliver—"

He broke off and stood waiting with a half angry, half baffled look; and then as she was still silent he picked up a red leather box from the table, laid it down again and came nearer to where she stood.

"Is it all a lie, Laura?" he demanded.

The justification which she had attempted alone in the night came back to her while she stood there with her hands, which felt like dead things, hanging limp at her sides. "It was so very little that it escaped my memory," was what she had said to herself in the darkness; but now, face to face with him in the light of day, she could not bring her mind to think these words nor her lips to utter them.

"No, it isn't a lie—it is true," she answered.

"It is true?" he repeated in an astonishment which gave place to anger as he went on. "Do you mean you really met her in my rooms?"

"I met her there—I met her there!" she rejoined in a bitter triumph of truth which seemed, somehow, a relief to her.

"And you did not tell me?"

She shook her head. "I'd never have told you."

"But the letter? What became of the letter?"

She had drawn a step away from him, not in any fresh spirit of evasion, but that she might gain a better view of the look with which he confronted her. Her eyes had not wavered from his since the first question he had asked, but her hands were nervously knotting and unknotting a silver cord which she had picked up from a jeweller's box upon the table at her side.

"Why didn't I get the letter, Laura?" he asked again.

"Because I burned it," she answered slowly, "I burned it in the fire in your room just before you came in—I burned it," she repeated for the third time, raising her voice to clearer distinctness.

A dark flush rose to his face and the sombre colour gave him an almost brutal look.

"In God's name why did you do it?" he asked; and she saw the contempt in his eyes as she had seen it before in her imagination. "I am to presume, I suppose, that you were prompted by jealousy?" he added. "An amiable beginning for a marriage."

"I don't know why I did it," she replied, in a voice which was so constrained as to sound unfeeling. "I didn't know at the time and I don't know now. Yes, I suppose jealousy is as good a reason as any other."

"And is this what I am to expect in the future?" he enquired, with an irony which he might as well have flung at a figure of wood. "Good God!" he exclaimed as his righteous resentment swept from his mind all recollection of his own relapses. "Are you willing to marry a man whom you can't trust out of your sight?"

The force with which he uttered the words drove them so deeply into his consciousness that he was convinced by his own violence of the justice in the stand he took. "Have you absolutely no faith in me?" he demanded.

For a moment the question occupied her thoughts.

"No, I don't think I have any now," she answered, "I've tried to make myself believe I had—I've told a lie to my conscience about it every day I lived—but I don't think I've ever really had faith in you since that night—"

"And yet you are willing to marry me?" he asked, and the scorn in his voice stung her like a physical blow. He looked at her with an angry glance, and while his eyes rested upon her, she understood that he had never really seen her in his life—that he had never penetrated beyond the outward aspect, the trick of gesture.

"No!—No!" she cried out suddenly, as if she had awakened in terror from her sleep. At the instant she saw herself through his eyes, humiliated, beaten down, unwomanly, and she was possessed by a horror of her own individuality which she felt in some way to be a part of her horror of the man who had revealed it to her.

In his perplexity he had fallen back a step and stood now pulling nervously at his moustache with a gesture which recalled his resemblance to Perry Bridewell. This gesture, more than any words he spoke, shocked her into an acuteness of perception which was almost unnatural in its vividness. It was as if her soul, so long drugged to insensibility, had started up in the last battle for liberation.

"No—no—it is impossible!" she repeated.

"Aren't you rather late in coming to this decision?" he enquired with a short laugh.

But his irony was wasted upon her, for she saw only the look in his eyes, which revealed her deception to her in a blaze of scorn—and she felt that she hated him and herself with an almost equal hatred.

"I am sorry, but—but I can't," she stammered. Feeling her words to be ineffectual she cast about wildly for some reason, some explanation however trivial—and in the effort she found her eyes wandering aimlessly about the room, taking in the scattered wedding presents, his dejected yet angry look, and the fading white rosebud Gerty had pinned jauntily in his coat. Then at last she realised that there was nothing further that she could say, so she stood helplessly knotting the silver cord while she watched the furious perplexity in which he tugged at his moustache.

"I can't for the life of me see why you should be so damned jealous, Laura," he burst out presently, thrust back from the surface conventions into a brute impulse of rage.

"I told you I didn't know," she answered irritably, "I told you that—"

"Of course, I'm willing to let it go this time," he went on, with what she felt to be a complacent return to his lordly attitude, "there's no use making a fuss, so we may as well forget it—but, for heaven's sake, don't give me a jealous wife. There's nothing under heaven more likely to drive a man insane."

Some elusive grace in her attitude—a suggestion of a wild thing poised for flight—arrested him suddenly as he looked at her; and she saw his face change instantly while the fire of passion leaped to his eyes.

"Be a darling and we'll forget it all!" he exclaimed.

He made a step forward, but shrinking back until she appeared almost to crouch against the wall, she put out her hands as if warding off his approach.

"Don't touch me!" she said; and though she spoke in a whisper, her words seemed to shriek back at her from the air. The thought that she was fighting for the freedom of her soul rushed through her brain, and at the instant, had he laid his hand upon her, she knew that she would have thrown herself from the window.

"I don't want to touch you," he returned, cooling immediately, "but can't you come to your senses and be reasonable?"

"If you don't mind I wish you'd go," she said, looking at him with a smile which was like the smile of a statue.

"If I go now will you promise to get sensible again?" he asked, with annoyance, for it occurred to him that since he had made up his mind to be magnanimous, she had repulsed his generosity in a most ungrateful fashion.

"I am sensible," she responded, "I am sensible for the first time for months."

"Well, you've a pretty way of showing it," he retorted. His irritation got suddenly the better of him, and fearing that it might break out in spite of his control, he turned toward the door. "For God's sake, let's make the best of it now," he added desperately.

In his nervousness he stumbled against the table and upset the red leather box which contained the coffee service.

"I beg your pardon," he said, and stooping to pick it up, he replaced the silver in the case before he went into the hall and closed the door behind him.

CHAPTER III
PROVES A GREAT CITY TO BE A GREAT SOLITUDE

After he had gone Laura remained standing where he had left her, until the sound of the hall door closing sharply caused her to draw a breath of relief as if there had come a temporary lifting of the torture she endured. Then, with her first movement, as she looked about the room in the effort to bring order into the confusion of her thoughts, her eyes encountered the array of wedding presents, and the expression of her face changed back into the panic terror in which she had couched against the wall before Kemper's approach. She still saw herself revealed in the light of the scorn which had blazed in his eyes; and the one idea which possessed her now was to escape beyond the place where that look might again reach her. An instinct for flight like that of a wild thing in a jungle shook through her until she stood in a quiver from head to foot; and though she knew neither where she was going, nor of what use this flight would be to her, she went into her bedroom and began to dress herself hastily in her walking clothes. As she tied on her veil and took up her little black bag from the drawer she heard her own voice, which sounded to her ears like the voice of a stranger, repeating the words she had said to Kemper a little earlier: "No—no—I cant. It is impossible." And she said over these words many times because they infused into her heart the courage of despair which she needed to impel her to the step before her. When the door closed after her and she went down into the street, she was still speaking them half aloud to herself: "No—no—it is impossible."

The dusk had already settled; ahead of her the lights of the city shone blurred through the greyness, while above the housetops Auriga was driving higher in the east. With the first touch of fresh air in her face, she felt herself inspired by an energy; which seemed a part of the wind that blew about her; and as she walked rapidly through streets which she did not notice toward an end of which she was still ignorant, her thoughts breaking from the restraint which held them, rushed in an excited tumult through her brain.

"Why did he look at me so?" she asked, "for it is this look which has driven me away—which has made me hate both him and myself." She tried to recall the other expression which she had loved in his face, but instead there returned to her only the angry look with which he had responded to her confession.

As she thought of it now it appeared to her that death was the only means by which she could free herself and him from this marriage; and the several ways of dying which were possible to her crowded upon her with the force of an outside pressure. She might be crushed in the street? or walk on till she found the river? But the different approaches to death showed to her as so hideous that she knew she could not summon the courage with which to select a particular one and follow it to the end. "Yet I shall never go back," she thought, "he does not love me—he wishes only to spare himself the scandal. If he loved me he could never have looked at me like that. And I loved him three weeks ago," she added. Her love was gone now, and the memory of it had become intolerable to her, yet the vacancy where it had been was so great that death occurred to her again as the only outcome. "Though I hate him it seems impossible that I should live on without him," she said.

But the next instant when she endeavored to recall his face she could remember him only by his casual likeness to Perry Bridewell, and she saw him standing upon the hearthrug while he pulled in angry perplexity at his moustache. The words he had spoken, the tones of his voice, and her own emotion, were blotted from her recollection as if a thick darkness had wiped them out, and from the hour of her deepest anguish she could bring back only a meaningless gesture and the white rosebud he had worn in his coat. What she had suffered then was the dying agony of the thing within her which was really herself, and there remained to her now only the vacant image from which the passion and the life had flown. "How could it make so much difference when I can barely remember it?" she asked; and it seemed to her at the instant that nothing that could happen in one's existence really mattered, since big and little were all equal, and the memory of an emotion faded sooner than the memory of a gesture.

Pausing for a moment on the corner, she watched curiously the faces moving under the electric lights, and she found herself wondering presently if each man or woman in the crowd was loving and hating or seeking an escape from both love and hatred? A stout man wearing a red necktie, a pretty woman in a purple coat, a pale girl carrying a heavy bundle, a bent shouldered clerk who walked with a satisfied and affected air—as each one passed she saw his features and even his hidden thoughts in a grotesque clearness which seemed to come partly from an illumination within herself and partly from the glare of the lights without. "The man in the red necktie is happy because he has made money; the pretty woman is happy because she is loved—but the pale girl and the bent shouldered clerk are wretched. They have neither love nor money, and they have not found out how little either is worth."

For a while she watched them, almost forgetting her own unhappiness in the excitement of their discovered histories; but wearying suddenly, she turned away and entered a street where the darkness had already gathered. Here she came close upon a pair of lovers who walked arm in arm, but the sight irritated her so she turned again at the next corner. The question whether she should go home or not thrust itself upon her, and it seemed to her that it would be better to die in the street than to return to the persuasions of Gerty, the reproaches of Mrs. Payne, and the complacency of Kemper. As she hurried on in the darkness she saw her past as distinctly as if her eyes were turned backward, and in this vision of it there showed to her the steep upward way of the spirit, and she remembered the day when her destiny had seemed to lie mapped out for her in the hand of God. "Was this what God meant?" she demanded, and because there was no answer to the question she asked it again and again the more passionately. "Or perhaps there is no God after all," she added.

A sob broke from her lips, and a policeman, who was passing, threw first an enquiring, then a respectful glance at her, and went on again. A child playing in the street ran up to beg for some money, and she opened her bag and gave him a piece of silver with a smile.

"Thank you, lady," he responded, and ran back into the shadows. As he crossed the street she followed him with her eyes, seeing him hasten, his palm outstretched, to an Italian who was roasting chestnuts in a charcoal burner on the opposite sidewalk.

The darkness had grown heavier and as she walked rapidly through streets which she did not know, her nervous energy failed her, and she began to tremble presently from exhaustion. Again she asked herself for the last time if it were possible for her to go home and face Mrs. Payne and Gerty and marry Kemper in three days. A fantastic humour in the situation brought a laugh to her lips—for whenever she was confronted by the hopelessness of her escape, the arguments for her marriage presented themselves to her in the forms of cases of silver and of her wedding dress in its white satin box. Mrs. Payne had spent the afternoon, she knew, in arranging this silver on covered tables in an empty room, and she could see plainly the old lady's animated movements, the careful eye with which she estimated the value of each gift, and the expression of approval or contempt with which she grouped it according to its importance. Then she thought of Kemper held to his love by the embarrassment of these presents, by the hopelessness of returning them, and by his conventional horror of "getting into print," and at the picture the laugh grew almost hysterical on her lips. How sordid it all was! This array of silver, Mrs. Payne's reproachful comic mask, and Kemper, pulling his moustache as he stood upon the hearthrug, all whirled confusedly in the dimly lighted street before her. She felt her knees tremble, and while this weakness lasted it seemed to her that it would be better to go back and get warm again, and submit to anything they forced upon her. Her flesh, in its weakness, would have yielded, but something more powerful than the flesh—the soul within which she had so long rejected—struggled on after the impulses of the body had surrendered.

The lights grew suddenly blurred before her eyes, and looking up, she found that she had reached a ferry, and that a crowd from a neighbouring factory was hurrying through the open doors into the boat which was about to put off. For the first time it occurred to her that she might leave the city; and going inside she bought a ticket and followed the people who were rushing across the gangway. Where it would take her she had no idea, but when after a few minutes the boat had crossed to the other side, she went out again with the crowd, and then turning in the direction where there appeared to be open country, she walked on more rapidly as if her thoughts flew straight ahead into the broader spaces of the horizon.

At first there were rows of streets, a few scattered shops in among the houses, and groups of workmen from the factories lounging upon the sidewalk. A child, with a crooked back, in a red dress, ran across the pavement in front of her and stopped with an exclamation before a window which contained a display of pink and white candy. Then a second child joined her, and the two fell to discussing the various highly coloured sweets arrayed on little fancy squares of paper behind the glass. As Laura watched them, pausing breathlessly in her walk, every trivial detail of this incident seemed to her to possess an equal importance with all other happenings large or small: for the events of her individual experience had so distorted her perceptions of the ascending values of life, that her own luckless pursuit of happiness appeared of no greater importance in her eyes than the child, with the crooked back, making her choice of sweets. Her own emotions, indeed, interested her no longer, but she was aware of a dull curiosity concerning the crippled child. Would her whole life become misshapen because of the physical form which she wore like an outer garment? And she felt, at the thought, that she would like to stand upon the side of the child and upon the side of all who were oppressed and made miserable by the crookedness either of the body or of destiny.

While this pity was still in her mind she tried to recall Kemper as she had first known him, but it was to remember only that he had reddened with anger as he spoke to her, and that the sunlight, falling upon him, had revealed the gray hair on his temples. The physical aspect which had meant so little in her love was all that the recollection of him could suggest to her now, for she found that the visual memory still remained after the passion which had informed it with life and colour was blotted out.

The child interested her no longer, and walking on again, she passed, after a time, the scattered houses, and came out upon the open road which showed white and deserted beneath the stars. Looking overhead, as she went on, her gaze swept the heavens with that sense of absolute stillness which comes under the solitude of the sky, and standing presently in the dust of the road, she fixed her eyes upon the Pleiades shining softly far above the jagged line of the horizon. Her feet ached beneath her, but her head seemed suddenly spinning through clear spaces among the stars, and while she stood there, she felt that the distance between her and the sky existed only in the hindrance of her body. With that laid aside might she not recover her soul and God there as well as here?

Again she went on, but this time she found that her limbs could make no further effort, and struggling step by step, to a bend in the road, she looked about her in a physical agony which left her consciousness only of her desire for rest. A house, set back from the roadside in a clump of trees, showed to her as she turned, and going through the little whitewashed gate and up the path, she knocked at the door and then stood trembling before the threshold.

CHAPTER IV
SHOWS THAT TRUE LOVE IS TRUE SERVICE

On the evening of the day upon which Laura was to have been married, Adams went, as usual, into his study and lit the green lamp upon his desk; but his mind was so filled with the mystery of her absence that even the pretence of distraction became unendurable. Since the news of her broken engagement and her flight had reached him, he had spent three days in a fruitless, though still hopeful, search for her; and the nights when he was forced to relax his efforts were filled with agonised imaginings of her loneliness at so great a distance and yet in reality so near. From the moment that he had heard through Gerty of her disappearance, there had ceased to exist all uncertainty as to the position in which he now stood to her; and he reproached himself, as he remembered her visit to his office, because he had failed then to take into his hands a decision which from an external view appeared so little to affect him.

But the external view, he realised, was nothing to him to-night. On that last day he had penetrated beneath the shallow surface of the conventions, and he had read in her tormented heart the whole story of the bitter disillusionment which she did not dare to put in words. Her imagination, he saw, had created an ideal lover in Kemper's shape, and in the moment of her awakening she had turned away not from the falsehood, but from the truth. "Though he is not what I loved yet I will still love him!" her heart had cried, in a subjection to the old false feminine belief that faithfulness to a mistaken ideal is not weakness but virtue. Yet in the end she had fled from that ultimate choice between the higher and the lower nature. How could she have lived on a lie when her spirit had forged so clear a path of truth before her?

Rising from his chair he walked for a few minutes rapidly up and down the room. How far or how near was she to-night? Had she remembered him in her misery? Would God reveal Himself to her in the most terrible hour? His trust in her final deliverance was so great that even as he put the questions, he knew in his heart that she was one of those who, in the end, "win their own souls through perseverance." His eyes fell on her picture above his desk, and then turning away rested on Connie's which stood where he had placed it in the first years of his marriage. Connie and her life with him was like a half-forgotten dream to him now, yet, looking back upon it, he could not tell himself that there had been for him no gain of strength, for Connie no growth of understanding, in the pitiless failure of their marriage. All was softened in his memory by that last afternoon when he had seen the shame of experience wiped from her face as they combed her hair straight back from her forehead in the old childish fashion; and he had realised from that instant that a soul had come to birth in the hour before her death. A single ray of the divine light had dispelled the thick darkness, and her blind eyes were opened for one minute before she closed them to the body forever. Was that one minute not worth every heart throb he had suffered and every difficult hope for which he had battled in his thoughts? Having looked though for a fleeting glimpse only upon the unity of life, was not her spirit's growth measured in the instant of that flashing vision? For God had worked here—had worked in the pity of his heart, as well as in the awakening gratitude in Connie's; and because of the deeper insight he had attained, he could look back over the whole sordid tragedy and discern one of those steep and arduous roads by which the spirit mounts to enlightenment through the flesh. And if this were so here—if in ugliness such as this he could find beauty, was it not one and the same over the broad field of human effort? Had not his own life proved to him that let a man's eyes be opened, and even in the depths of abasement he may look in his soul and discover God?

And Laura? His heart was flooded with tenderness, and he felt again a confident, an almost mystic assurance that her destiny was one with his. In this growing conviction his anxiety appeared to him suddenly as a pitiable and cowardly denial of his faith—and he was possessed by the certainty that he had only to send out his will in order to smooth the way of her return to peace.

The room had become warm, and opening the window he stood looking beyond the housetops to the stars which shone dimly over the city. The noise in the streets grew fainter in his ears, and as he stood there with his eyes on the stars, he could tell himself in the joy of his reconciliation, that the law by which they moved gloriously toward their end was the law which controlled his own and Laura's life. The sense which is less a belief than an intimate knowledge of immortality belonged to him now, and he realised that so far as he lived at all he lived not in the hour alone, but in eternity, that so far as he had won peace it was bound up in a passionate conviction of the survival of the universe within his soul. To-day or to-morrow, in the minute or in eternity, he saw that wherever God is there will always be immortal life.

Turning back into the room he looked again at Laura's picture with a longing which had not freed itself as yet from the idea of renouncement. Even now he realised that he had been strong enough to live without her, and with the admission, he was aware again of that wider sympathy which had been his compensation in a forefeiture of personal love. His happiness he had told himself a year ago depended neither upon possession nor upon any passage of events, yet to-night his heart strained after her in a tenderness which seemed to bring her visible presence before him in the room. His love for her appeared not only as a part of his love for God, but as a part, also, of his sorrows, his bitter patience, his renouncement and of the compassion which had sprung from the agony and the enlightenment of his failure. Sorrow he could still feel—the deepest human grief might be his portion to-morrow, but while this unfading light shone in his soul, he knew that it was ordained that he should conquer in the end. By this knowledge alone he had at last won through suffering into the open places of the spirit where were joy and freedom.

A ring at the bell startled him from his abstraction, and with an impatient eagerness for news, he hastened to the door, where a boy thrust at him a small folded sheet of paper. As he opened it he felt that his hand trembled, for even before he read the words, he knew that Laura's appeal to him had come.

"I need a friend. Will you help me?" was all that she had written.

He motioned the boy to come inside, and then stood looking at him enquiringly as he got into his overcoat.

"Do you go back with me?" he asked.

The boy nodded while he pulled at a scarlet handkerchief about his neck. Adams noticed that though he was stunted and anæmic in appearance, he wore his shabby overcoat with an almost rakish swagger. His mouth was filled with chewing-gum which he rolled aside in his cheek when he talked.

"Is it far?" Adams enquired in a hopeless effort to extort information however meagre.

The boy looked important, almost mysterious.

"Yep," he responded, adding immediately, "She's the other side of the ferry."

"Do you mean the lady?" He opened the door, and hurried to the sidewalk where he stopped to call a cab from the corner.

"She's been there three nights, so tired she couldn't move," replied the boy, as he followed Adams into the cab. "A fine lady, too," he commented with a wink.

"Well, she's all right now, and I'm much obliged to you," said Adams, but he asked no further questions until they were seated side by side in the ferry, when he tried again to draw out the bare facts of Laura's flight.

During the walk through the town and along the country road, he learned that Laura had reached the house of the boy's mother in an exhaustion of mind and body which had compelled them to harbour her for the night. On the next day her appearance and the money with which she was supplied had so won upon the mother's sympathy that her desire to remain a few days longer had been met almost with eagerness by the older woman. When he had, with difficulty, extracted this account of what had passed, Adams fell a little ahead of his companion, and they went on in silence until they came, at the end of several miles, in sight of the cottage withdrawn from the roadside in its clump of trees. A single lighted window was visible through the bared boughs, and standing out clearly from the interior, Adams saw a dark figure which his heart recognised with a bound.

The boy pushed back the gate and Adams went up the path inside, and entering the house opened the door of the room in which he had seen Laura standing. She was still there, motionless in the lamplight, and as he went toward her she lifted her eyes and gazed back at him in the mute defiance which is the outward expression of despair.

"Do you think you have been quite just to me, Laura?" he asked, not tenderly, but with a stern and reproachful face.

Without lowering her eyes she looked at him while she shook her head.

"I sent for you because I could not help it. I had nowhere to go," she said.

"Do you think you have been just to me?" he asked again.

"You? I never thought of you until to-day," she answered. "I came here because I had to go somewhere—it did not matter where. I was too tired to walk any farther, so they were very good to me."

"And you have let us search for you three days." His voice was constrained, but as he looked into her wan face between the loosened waves of her hair, his heart melted over her in an agony of tenderness. Every drop of blood appeared to have left her body, which was so pallid that he seemed to see the light shining through her drawn features.

"So they have been looking for me?" she observed, with but little interest.

"What did you expect?" he questioned in his turn.

"But I didn't want to be found—I would rather stay lost," she responded. Shrinking away from him she went to the window and stood there, pressed closely against the panes, as if in a blind impulse to put the space of the room between them. "I will not go back even now—I will not go back," she insisted.

As he entered he had closed the door behind him, and leaning against it now, he looked at her with a flicker of his quiet smile.

"I'm not talking about going back, am I?" he rejoined. "Heaven knows you may stay here if you like the place." He glanced quickly about the crudely furnished little room hung with cheap crayon portraits. "It's rather hard, though, to fit you into these surroundings," he remarked with a flash of humour.

She shook her head. "They suit me as well as any other."

"And the people who live here?—What of them?"

"I like them because they are so near to the ground," she answered, "they've no surface of culture, or personality, or convention to bother one—they've no surface, indeed, of any kind."

"Well, it's all very interesting," he remarked, smiling, "but, in common decency, don't you think you might have sent me word?"

"I never thought of you an instant," she replied.

"You never thought of me in your life," he retorted, "and yet when I say I'm better worth your thinking of than Kemper—God knows I don't pretend to boast."

A weaker man would have hesitated over the name, but he had seen at the first glance that the way to save her was not by softness, and his lips, after he had uttered the word, closed tightly like the lips of a surgeon who applies the knife.

"Don't speak to me of him!" she cried out sharply, "I had forgotten!"

Her eyes hung upon his in a returning agony, and it was through this agony alone that he hoped to bring back her consciousness of life.

"This is not the way to forget," he answered, "you are not a coward, yet you have chosen the cowardly means. There can he no forgetfulness until you are strong enough to admit the truth to your own heart—to say 'there is no mistake that is final, no wrong done that has power to crush me.'"

"But there is no truth in my heart," she answered, with sudden energy, "it is all a lie—I am a lie all over, and it makes no difference because I have ceased to care. I used to think that people only died when they were put in coffins, but I know now that you can be dead and yet move and walk about and even laugh and pretend to be like all the rest—some of whom are dead also. And I didn't die slowly," she added, with a vague impersonal interest, which impressed him as almost delirious in its detachment, "I wasn't killed in a year, but in a minute. One instant I was quite alive—as alive as you are now—and the next I was as dead as if I had been buried centuries ago."

"And who is to blame for this?" he demanded, white to the lips.

"Oh, it wasn't he—it was life," she went on calmly, "he couldn't help it, nor could I—nobody can help anything. Do you understand that?" she asked, with the searching mental clearness which seemed always lying behind her dazed consciousness, "that we're all drawn by wires like puppets, and the strongest wire pulls us in the direction in which we are meant to go? It's curious that I should never have known this before because it has become perfectly plain to me now—there is no soul, no aspiration, no motive for good or evil, for we're every one worked by wires while we are pretending to move ourselves."

"All right, but it's my turn at the wire now," responded Adams, smiling.

At his words she broke out into little hard dry sobs, which had in them none of the softness of tears. "Nobody is to blame for anything," she repeated, still striving, in a dazed way, to be just to Kemper.

Even more than her face and her voice, this pathetic groping of her reason, moved him into a passion of sympathy; and while he looked at her, he resisted an impulse to gather her, in spite of her coldness, against his breast.

"What is it, Laura, that has made you suffer like this?" he asked.

But his words made no impression upon her, perhaps because they could not penetrate the outer husk of deadness which enveloped her.

"Do you know what it is to feel ashamed?" she demanded suddenly, "to feel ashamed, not in a passing quiver, but in a settled state every instant that you live? Do you know what it is to have every sensation of your body merged into this one feeling of shame—to be ashamed with your eyes and hands and feet as well as with your mind and heart and soul? I could have stood anything but this," she added, pressing closer against the window.

An exclamation which was almost one of anger burst from him, and going to where she stood, he laid his hand upon her arm as if in the effort to recall her reason by physical force. But with his first touch his grasp lost its energy and grew gentle, for her anguish appeared to him, as he held her, to be only the instinctive crying out of a child that is hurt. His hold slipped from her arm, and taking her hands, he bent over and kissed them until they lay quiet in his own.

"Laura, do you trust my love for you?" he asked.

"I trust you, yes," she answered, "but not love—it is only one of the wires by which we are moved."

"Trust anything you please about me, so long as you trust—that is all I ask," he let her hands fall from his and looked into her face. "Promise me that you will be here waiting when I return."

"There's no place for me to go—I shall be here," she answered.

Her eyes followed him with a pathetic child-like fear while he crossed the room and went out leaving her alone.

CHAPTER V
BETWEEN LAURA AND GERTY

Did he possess the strength as well as the love that she needed? Adams asked himself a little later as he walked back under the stars. He saw her as he had just left her—wan, despairing; so bloodless that the light seemed shining through her features, and then he remembered the radiant smile which she had lost, the glorious womanhood obscured now by humiliation. An assurance, in which there was almost exultation, flooded his thoughts, and he was aware that the passion he felt for her had been suddenly strengthened by an emotion of equal power—by the longing born in his heart to afford protection to whatever suffered within his sight.

Never for an instant, since he had entered the room where she retreated before him, had he doubted either his appointed mission or his power of renewal. His whole experience, he understood now, had directed him to this hour which he had not foreseen, and the worldly success for which he had once struggled meant to him at last only that he might bring hope where there was failure. Even Connie—her love, her tragic history, her pitiable reliance upon him at the end—showed to him in the aspect of a human revelation—for his fuller understanding of Connie had confirmed him in the patience by which alone he might win back Laura to the happiness which she had lost.

The road stretching ahead of him was no longer obscured, but shone faintly luminous out of the surrounding darkness. Not the future alone but the desert places through which he had come had blossomed, and the beauty which was revealed to him at last was the beauty in all things that have form or being—in the earth no less than in the sky, in the flesh no less than in the spirit, for were not earth and flesh, after all, only sky and spirit in the making? The perfect plan, he had learned, in the end, is not for any part but for the whole.

Across the ferry, he found a cab which took him to Gerty's house, and in response to his message, she came down immediately, looking excited and perturbed, in an evening gown of black and silver.

"Have you brought me news of Laura?" she asked breathlessly. "Perry's dragging me to a dinner, but if she's ill, I can't go—I won't."

"Don't go," he answered, "she's not ill, but if she were it would be better. Will you come with me now and bring her back with you?"

Without replying to his question, she ran from the room and returned, in a moment, wearing a hat and a long coat which covered her black and silver dress.

"The carriage is waiting now," she said, "we can take it and let Perry go to his dinner in a cab."

"But—good Lord, Gerty—what am I to say to them?" demanded Perry while he shook hands with Adams. "I never could make up an excuse in my life, you know."

Then his eyes blinked rapidly and he fell back with merely a muttered protest, for Gerty shone, at the instant, with a beauty which neither he nor Adams had ever seen in her before. The wonderful child quality softened her look, and they watched her soul bloom in her face like a closed flower that expands in sunlight.

"I don't know, my dear," she responded gently, and with her hand on Adams's arm, she ran down the steps and into the carriage before the door. As they drove away, she looked up at him with a tender little smile.

"I am so glad that she has you," she said.

"In having you, she has a great deal more."

"It is you who have done it all—you expected me to have courage, so I have it. Had you expected me to be cowardly, I should have been so."

"Well, I expect you to save her," he answered quietly.

"Does she need it? What was it? What does it mean?"

"You'll know to-night, perhaps. I shall never know, but what does it matter?"

"I saw Arnold to-day," she said, "he is terribly—terribly—" she hesitated for a word, "cut up about it. Yet he swears he can't for the life of him see that he was to blame. Had he been to blame, he says, he would have shot himself."

"Would he?" he remarked indifferently.

"He sails for Europe on Saturday—if he hears she's found."

He bit back an exclamation of anger.

"What, under heaven, has he to do with it?" he asked.

"A great deal, one would think. But have you seen her? Tell me of her."

"Be good to her," he answered, "she is in a hard place and needs a great deal of love."

"And we can give it to her, you and I?"

"Mine is hers already, if it's any help."

"Was it hers before she knew Arnold even?"

"Long before—before he or you or I were born."

"And does she understand?"

"She doesn't know—but what difference does that make?"

Her eyes, in the flickering light, gave him an impression of remoteness as of dim stars.

"I wonder how it feels to be loved like that?" she said, a little wistfully.

"You would never have cared for it," he answered, with a flash of his penetrating insight, "for the kind of man who could have loved you in that way you couldn't have loved."

"You mean that I was born to adore the god in the brute?" she asked.

"Oh, well, so long as it's the god!" he retorted laughing.

But she paid no heed to his remark, and drawing her coat about her as if she were cold, she sat in silence until the carriage was driven upon the ferry and they began the trip across.

"She came this way all alone and at night?" she said.

"How or why we shall probably never know entirely," he answered. "I doubt if she realised herself where she was going."

"It looks meaningless from a distance, but, I suppose, in reality, it was a courageous flight?"

"Yes, I think there was courage in it," he responded quietly.

She turned her eyes away, looking out as they drove through the open country upon the black fields and the stars. Neither of them spoke again until the carriage stopped and the footman jumped down to ask for some directions. Then as they drew up presently before the little gate, Adams helped her out and along the path into the house.

"She is in there," he said, pointing to a closed door, "when you see her you will understand."

"But you will come, too?" she asked, hesitating.

He shook his head. "Her heart is bleeding—it's a woman that she wants."

Then he opened the door, and pushing her gently inside, closed it after her.

At first Gerty could see but faintly by the light of a lamp which smoked, but as she went quickly forward, Laura rose from the sofa upon which she had been lying, and came a step to meet her.

"Why did you come? I didn't want you—I didn't want anyone," she said.

Before the hard tones of her voice, Gerty stood still, shrinking slightly away in her baffled splendour. Her heart strained toward her friend, yet when she tried to think of some comforting word that she might utter, she found only a vacancy of scattered phrases. What would words mean to Laura now? What word among all others was there that she could speak to her?

For a moment, groping blindly for light, she hesitated; then her arms opened, and she caught Laura into them in spite of her feeble effort at resistance.

"Dearest! dearest! dearest!" she repeated, for she had found the word at last.

Partly because she was a woman and partly because of her bitter triumphs, she had understood that the wisdom in love is the only wisdom which avails in the supreme agony of life. Neither philosophy nor religion mattered now, for presently she felt that her bosom was warm with tears, and when Laura lifted her head, the two women kissed in that intimate knowledge which is uttered without speech.

CHAPTER VI
RENEWAL

In that strange spiritual death—which was still death though the members of her body lived—Laura seemed to lose gradually all personal connection with the events through which she had passed; and when after three months she turned again to look back upon them, she found that they stood out, clear, detached, and remote as the incidents of history. She was not only dead herself, but the whole world about her showed to her in a curious aspect of unreality, as if a thin veil obscured it, and there were moments when even Adams and Gerty seemed to her to be barely alive. To the last she had refused to return to Gramercy Park, and on the night that she reached Gerty's house she had been aware that she was slipping away from any actual contact with her former life. Her body might breathe and move, but her soul and even her senses had become inanimate, and she felt that they had ceased to take part in any words she uttered.

Though she had persistently denied herself to her aunts, she sent for Mr. Payne on the first day that she was able to sit up, and the only softness she showed was in answer to the compassionate kiss he placed upon her forehead.

"My child, my child, what did I tell you?" he asked gently.

"It is because of that I wanted to see you," she said, "because you are the only person, I believe, who can really understand."

"I think I can, my dear."

"You have had beautiful dreams, too, that were false ones?"

"It isn't that the dreams are false," he replied, "but that the stuff of this earth isn't the kind to grow illusions. They must either wither in the bud or be wrenched up root and branch."

"And there's only the ugly reality, after all?"

"There's only the reality, but it isn't ugly when one grows accustomed to it. You'll find it good enough for you yet, my child."

"No—no," she said, "I've always lived on pretty lies, I see that now—I've always had to find an outlet for my imagination, however false. My poetry was never more than this—it was all quotation—all a reflection of the things I had wanted to feel in life. I never wrote a sincere line," she added.

He pressed her hand—it was his way of showing that he loved her none the less because she was not a poet—and then as the unnatural wanness overspread her face, he went out softly, leaving her in Gerty's care. By different roads they had come at last to the same place in life—she with her blighted youth and he with his beautiful old age and his disappointed hopes.

With the beginning of the year Gerty went South with her, but the soft air or the cold made little difference to Laura, when, as she said, she could feel neither. There had been no outburst of grief; since the night when she had wept on Gerty's bosom, she had not shed a tear; and once when Gerty had alluded to Kemper in her hearing, she had listened with the polite attention she might have bestowed upon the name of a stranger. At Gerty's bidding she came or went, admired or disapproved, but of her old impulsive energy there was so little left that Gerty sometimes wondered if her friend had really, as she insisted, "turned to stone." For Laura's face even had frozen until it wore the impassive smile of a statue, and there was in her movements and her voice something of the insensibility of extreme old age. She was no longer young, nor was she middle-aged; it was as if she had outlived, not only the emotions, but the years of life.

In April they came back again, and on the morning after their return Gerty paid a dejected visit to Adams in his office.

"I can do nothing with her—she's turned to stone," she said.

"Oh, she'll come alive again," he responded. "Where is she?"

"In Gramercy Park. It makes no difference to her now where she is, nor whether she sees Mrs. Payne or not. She even sits for hours and listens to Uncle Percival play upon his flute."

"It will be the death of her," he answered gravely. "Is there nothing we can do?"

"Nothing. I've done everything—she's really stone."

"Well, we'll bring her round," said Adams cheerfully; but when he saw Laura herself in the afternoon, he instinctively turned his eyes away from the frozen sweetness in her look. He was aware that she made an effort to be pleasant, but her pleasantness reminded him of an artificial light on a figure of snow.

“I had hoped you would grow stronger in the South,” he said, though all conversation seemed to him to have become suddenly the most impersonal thing on earth.

“But I am strong,” she answered, “I am never ill a day.”

“There’s something about you, all the same, that I don’t like,” he responded frankly.

“I know,” she nodded, smiling, “you aren’t used to seeing a dead person walk about. But it’s very comfortable when you grow accustomed to it,” she added, with a laugh.

At this he would have brought a more intimate note into his voice, but she evaded his first hint of earnestness by a cynical little jest she had picked up from Gerty. Her intention—if she intended anything—he saw clearly now was to confine her perceptions to the immediate surface of life presented before her eyes. She spoke with animation of the country she had left, of Gerty’s gayeties, of the wonderful brightness of the weather; but when by a more serious question he sought to penetrate below this fluency of words, he was repelled again by the impression of a mere hollow amiability in her manner. After a few casual remarks he left her with the most hopeless feeling he had known for months, and when, as the days went on, he endeavored fruitlessly to arouse in her a single sincere interest in human affairs, he found himself wondering if it were possible for any creature to be still alive and yet to resemble so closely a figure of marble. Day after day he came only to yield at last to his baffled efforts; and the thin cold smile with which she responded to his words appeared to him sadder than any passionate outburst of tears. Even Connie on that last afternoon had seemed to him more human and less unapproachable than Laura now.

Through the spring he saw her almost every day, and when in June he put her on the train with Gerty for the Adirondacks, he came away with the clutch, as if from a hand of ice, at his heart. He had given her his best and yet he had not penetrated by word or look beneath the unnatural gentleness which enveloped her like an outer covering. Then his heart hardened and he felt that he cursed Kemper for the thing which he had killed.

Back again in the forest, under the green and gold of the leaves, Laura asked herself why the associations of that last summer failed so strangely to disturb her as she looked on the familiar road and mountains? A single year or a whole lifetime ago, it was all one to her now, and while she wandered along the paths down which she had walked with Kemper in the most blissful hours of her love, she found herself almost regretting that she had ceased to suffer—that since her heart was broken it had lost even the power to throb. In the city she had felt herself to be a part of the houses and the streets, and as perfectly indifferent to the passage of life as they; but here with her heart against Nature's she would have liked to pulsate with the other live things in the forest. For the first time for months she began as the days went by, to quicken to an interest in the songs of the birds, or the sunsets on the mountains, or the springing up of a new flower beside the doorstep. And as in every rebound of the emotions from extreme despair, her connection with life came at last through the eye of the mind rather than through the heart, and the lesson was taught her neither by Gerty nor by Adams, but through an awakening to the beauty in the sights and the sounds of the green natural world about her.

Gerty had left her one afternoon, and as the cart drove away she went out of the house and sat down in the sun upon the roadside which bordered the edge of the wood. Behind her was the silence of the forest, and straight ahead the faint purple hills rose against a pale sky above which the white clouds sailed like birds. For a while she gazed with blind eyes at the view for the sake of which the spot was chosen, but the mountains and the sky left her unmoved, and leaning her arm presently upon the warm earth, she lay looking at a little blue flower blooming in the sand at her feet. Her shadow stretched beside her in the road, and it seemed to her that there was as little difference, save in her consciousness, between her and her shadow, as there was between her shadow and the flower. Even her love and her disillusion showed to her now as of no larger consequence than the wind blowing upon her shadow or the dew and the storm falling upon the flower. Then as the minutes passed and her gaze did not waver from the blue petals filled with sunshine, she was aware gradually, as if between dream and waking, of a peculiar deepening of her mental vision, until there was revealed to her, while she looked, not only the outward semblance, but the essence of the flower which was its soul. And this essence of the flower came suddenly in contact with the dead soul within her bosom, while she felt again the energy which is life flowing through her body. At this instant, by that divine miracle of resurrection she began to live anew—to live not her old life alone, but a life that was larger and fuller than the one which had been hers. She began to live anew in herself as well as in the sky and in humanity and in the songs of birds; and in this ecstasy of recovered life, she felt her soul to be of one substance, not only with God and the stars, but with the flower and the child in the street as well. For that love which had recoiled from its individual object overflowed her heart again until she felt that it had touched the boundaries of the world.

When Adams saw her in the autumn, he discovered the change almost with the first touch of her hand. Not only the outward form, but the indwelling intellect was alive again, and all that reminded him of her past anguish were a deeper earnestness in her smile and a faint powdering of silver on the dark wing-like waves of her hair. That veiled joy which is the expression of the soul that has found peace shone in her face with a radiance which if less bright was to him more beautiful than the sparkling energy she had lost. For the life and the passion of her womanhood were still there, mellowed and ennobled by that shadow of experience without which mere beauty of feature had always seemed to him a meaningless and empty shape. His belief was justified forever in that instant, and he recognised in her then one of those nobler spirits who in passing through the tragedy of disillusionment drain from it the strength without the bitterness that is its portion.

"I want to work, to help," she said eagerly, almost with her first breath, and while he listened with a tenderness tinged with amusement, she described to him the elaborate plans she had made for going among the poor. "It isn't that the poor need help any more than the rich," she added, "but the poor are the only ones that I can reach."

He nodded, smiling, while he watched the animated gestures of her hands. Her poetry, her groping for love, her longing at last to give help to the oppressed, each phase of thought or feeling through which she had passed, showed to him only as the effort of the soul within her to find expression. In this passionate search after the eternal upon earth was she not, in reality, only seeking in outward forms the thing which was herself?

"I will help you, of course," he answered, with a gravity which he found it difficult afterward to maintain, for from that moment she had thrown her heart into the work of uplifting until her whole existence appeared to round presently about this new point of interest. While he could follow her here, he waited almost impatiently for the reaction of her temperament which would bring her back to him, he felt, as inevitably as the changes of the seasons would bring the spring again to the earth.

On Christmas Eve she had arranged for some celebration among the poor on the East Side, and when they came away together, she asked him to take her to Gerty's house instead of to Gramercy Park. Then as they walked along the cross-town blocks from the elevated road, she alluded for the first time to the evening a year ago when he had found her in her deepest misery.

"I thought then that my life was over," she said, "but to-day I have put my foot upon my old grief and it has helped me to spring upward. The world is so full for me now that I can hardly distinguish among so many vivid interests—and yet nothing in it is changed except myself. Do you know what it is to feel suddenly that you have found the key?"

"I know," he replied, "for I have found it, too, and it is love."

"Love for the world—for all mankind," she corrected. "No, don't look at me like that," she added, "I am perfectly happy to-day, but it is the happiness of freedom."

For a moment he did not answer; then he turned his eyes upon the bright pallor of her cheek showing above the dark furs she wore, and there was a smile in his eyes though his voice, when he spoke, was grave.

"Do you know what I have sometimes thought about that, Laura," he said, "it is that I all along, from first to last, have known your heart better than you knew it for all your desperate certainty."

"I never knew it," she responded; "I do not know it now."

"And yet I think I do," he answered.

She shook her head. "It is no longer a mystery—there is only light in it to-day."

"I never thought you loved Kemper," he went on. "What you built your dream upon was an imaginary image that wore his shape. In my heart, even when I stood aside—when I was forced to stand aside because of other claims upon me—I think I was sure all the time that your love was meant for me at last."

"For you? Oh, no, not now," she answered.

"It's a bold way of saying it, I suppose," he pursued, "here I am neither rich nor successful as the world counts these things—in debt probably for several years to come, and with not so much as an athletic lustre to my name. It's not a cheerful picture I'm drawing, but because there's a struggle in it I am not afraid to ask you to come and share it. I wonder if you know how I have loved you, Laura."

"I have known since—since that night," she replied.

"The one argument I have to offer," he said, smiling, "is that in spite of the unpromising outlook, I happen to be the only man on earth who could make you happy."

"You might have been once," she responded.

"And if once, why not now? Is not forever as good as yesterday?"

"Do you know why?" she answered, turning upon him in sudden passion. "You think I am brave and yet I am afraid—afraid, though I won't admit it, every minute that I live. I walk the streets in terror of a memory."

"But I do not," he answered quietly. "Do you doubt my power to keep what I have won—my dearest?"

At the word the colour rose to her cheek, but as they reached Gerty's door, she stopped and put her hand into the one which he held out.

"Like everything else it has come too late," she said.

He shook his head, and then pressing her hand, let it fall.

"I can be patient a little longer," he responded before he turned away.

His words were still in her thoughts when she entered the house; and as she went quickly upstairs to Gerty's sitting-room, she wondered what counsel of indecision she would content herself with at last? Then as she crossed the threshold into the warm firelight, she discovered that Gerty was absent and that Arnold Kemper was standing upon the hearth rug.

As he recognised her he came forward, smiling, and held out his hand.

"So we've met again, after all, Laura," he remarked, without embarrassment.

At the sound of his voice there had come a single high throb of her heart and immediately afterward she was aware of an exultation which showed in the uplifting of her head and in her shining eyes—for as she looked into his face she measured for the first time the distance which divided her dream from her awakening.

"One always meets again, you know," she answered, "but if you're waiting for Gerty now, she is usually after time."

"Women always are," he commented gayly, with his foreign shrug.

The window was just behind him, and as he glanced out into the street, she looked at him in the puzzled wonder with which one seeks in unchanged features; a discernible justification of a passion which is altered. Where was the power to-day against which her heart had beat so helplessly a year ago? Was it possible that she had felt the charm in this man who was already middle-aged, who was satisfied with the mere concrete form of life, and in whose eyes she could see now the heaviness which grows through self-indulgence? His old intimate smile, his disturbing ironic glance, even the quickening of his first passive interest into the emotional curiosity which was the strongest impulse his world-weariness had left alive—each and all of these effects which she remembered impressed her as little to-day as did the bulky fascination of Perry Bridewell. When at last she could escape in the flutter of Gerty's entrance, she left the room and the house with a tremor of her pulses which was strangely associated with a delicious sense of peace—for this chance meeting had revealed to her not only Kemper but herself.

As she walked slowly toward the golden circle of the sky which was visible through the bared trees in the park, she recognised with every fibre of her body as unerringly as with her intellect that she had come at last into that knowledge which is the centre of outgoing life. And as Adams had seen in his deeper vision, that all life is an evolution into the consciousness of God, so she divined now through her mere vague instinct for light, that all emotion is but the blind striving of love after the consciousness of itself. Her whole experience flashed back before her, and in that swiftness of memory which prefigures either an accession of vitality or a tragic death, she understood that both her illusion and her disenchantment were necessary to the building of the structure within her soul. She had mounted by her mistake as surely as by her aspiration, and every pang which she had suffered was but the rending of the veil between her flesh and spirit.

Looking up as she walked she saw, without surprise, that Adams was standing under the bared trees before her; and with her first glance into his face she realised that there are moments charged with so deep a meaning that all explanations, all promises, all self-reproaches become only such vain and barren things as words.